YOUR TASK

Your task is to rescue your five friends and then find your way out of the Castle of Fear. Each time you choose a new path, you will be told which page to turn to next. But the wicked wizard has set many traps in the castle. Sometimes you can avoid them by finding your way through a maze or by finding something hidden in the picture. Often you have to use your wits. All you have to help you is a magic wish which you can use only once. Your sole companion is a monkey called Zetto who is not always very helpful! Whatever happens, you cannot turn back. Good luck!

First published 1986 by Walker Books Ltd
87 Vauxhall Walk, London SE11 5HJ

This edition published 2003

2 4 6 8 10 9 7 5 3 1

Text © 1986 Patrick Burston
Illustrations © 1986 Alastair Graham

The right of Patrick Burston and Alastair Graham to be identified as author and illustrator respectively of this work has been asserted by them in accordance with the Copyright, Designs and Patents Act 1988

This book has been typeset in Galliard

Printed in Hong Kong

British Library Cataloguing in Publication Data:
a catalogue record for this book is
available from the British Library

ISBN 0-7445-9465-0

THE CASTLE OF
FEAR

PATRICK BURSTON

illustrated by
ALASTAIR GRAHAM

WALKER BOOKS
AND SUBSIDIARIES
LONDON • BOSTON • SYDNEY

Here is the wizard's castle.
The drawbridge is down and
the lone sentry is fast asleep.
This is the moment for you and
Zetto to slip into the castle.

Now which way?
If you choose the left-hand
corridor turn to page 8.
If you choose the right-hand
corridor turn to page 10.

A cracked paving stone gives way
as Zetto touches it! All the cracked
paving stones are really trap-doors!
Find a safe way across the courtyard to one
of the staircases. (Trace a path with your finger.)

page 12 →

page 14 →

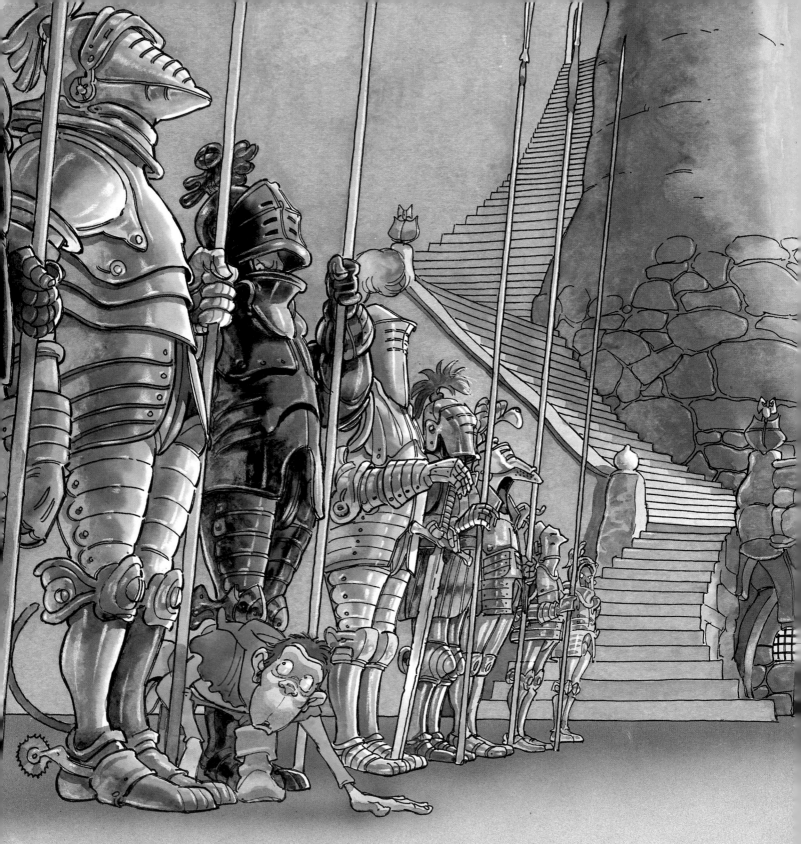

Careful! Guards are hiding in five of these suits of armour. You must spot them in order to avoid them.

Then if you choose the staircase turn to page 14. If you choose the banquet hall turn to page 16.

The stairs are blocked by eight terrifying ghosts conjured up by the wizard. Find four matching pairs and they will cancel each other out.

If you continue
down the stairs
turn to page 18.
Or use your magic
wish and turn to
page 20.

Trapped in a turret!
Can you find something
to help you get across to
one of those towers?

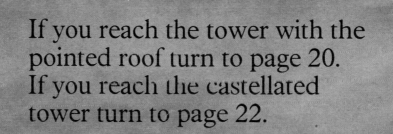

If you reach the tower with the pointed roof turn to page 20.
If you reach the castellated tower turn to page 22.

A delicious-looking feast! But the wizard has set many traps in this room. Can you spot eleven dangers to avoid? Then choose your way carefully. If you take the stairs behind the table turn to page 22. If you take the stairs on the right turn to page 24.

Five skeletons! Could they be your friends?
If the skeletons are human, your quest is in
vain! Study the bones before you go on.

If you choose to go up into the left eye-socket turn to page 28. If you go up into the right eye-socket turn to page 26.

You and Zetto are being attacked
by vampire bats. They are afraid
of light, so find something to smash
open the windows.

If you go down the stairs
turn to page 28.
If you go through the door
turn to page 30.

Five ghastly creatures are crawling up the walls of the tower. There's a bow handy – can you find one arrow to kill each creature?

Now which way? If you decide to dive into the moat turn to page 32.

If you choose to climb down the rungs set into the tower turn to page 30.

What a view! But the wizard's victims can't enjoy it because they have been turned into stone gargoyles. You will become a gargoyle too unless you smash that uncarved stone. What can you use?

Now which way?
If you choose to go through
the door turn to page 34.
If you decide to dive into
the moat turn to page 32.

Here are your five friends, imprisoned in a frightful torture chamber! Find five keys to release them.

You have released everyone but can you lead them to safety? Which way?
If you take the tunnel turn to page 44.
If you take the stairs turn to page 36.

You have discovered an electrified monster created by the wizard. Three of the four wires that activate him are broken; one wire is still connected to a switch. Find it and turn off the power before the monster kills you.

More confusing stairs! Which way?
If you take the left-hand archway
turn to page 38.
If you take the right-hand archway
turn to page 42.

If you take the left-hand archway turn to page 38. If you take the right-hand archway turn to page 42.

Poisonous fumes tell you it
would be fatal to fall into this
chasm beneath the castle.
Find a safe way across it.
(Trace a path with your finger.)

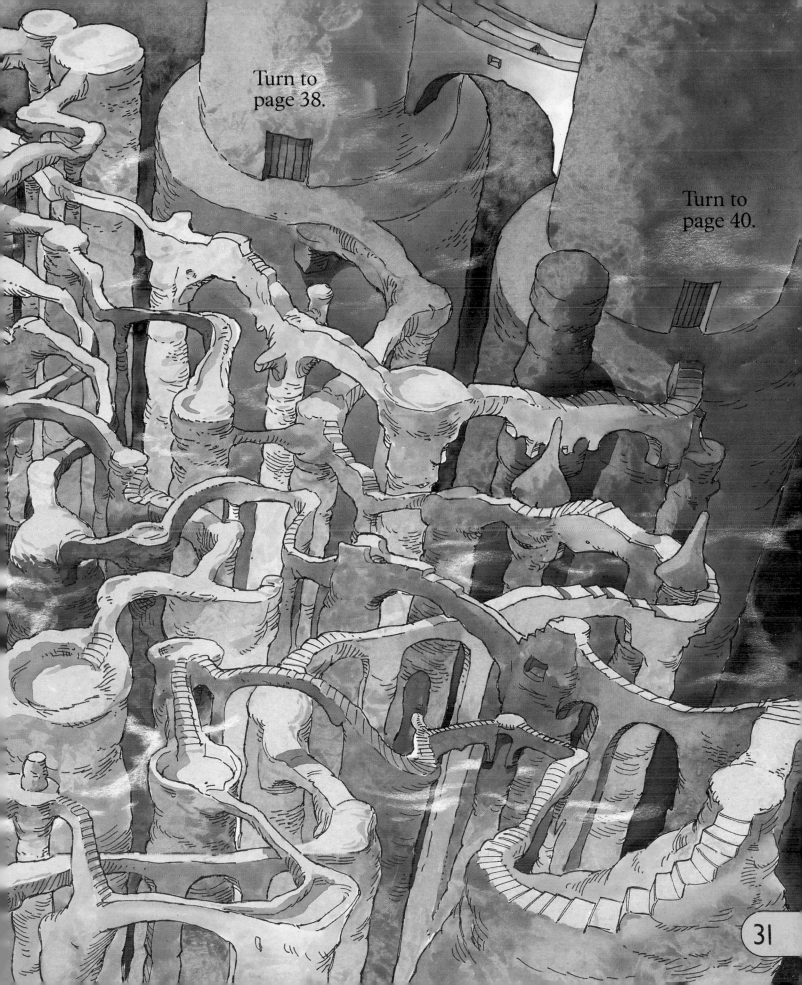

Turn to page 38.

Turn to page 40.

The castle guards have seen you
and Zetto dive into the moat!
Find a breathing tube so you
can swim away under water.

If you swim into the tunnel and
go up the steps turn to page 42.
If you swim further along the
tunnel turn to page 40.

You and Zetto are held in the spell of a magic mirror. Find nine differences between the image and its reflection before you are free of the spell.

Then you can step through the doorway reflected in the mirror (turn to page 42) or you can go through the real doorway (turn to page 38).

Disaster! Your friends have been recaptured and you have been thrown into a dungeon with thirty starving rats. Find a hungry cat for every five rats and you will be safe. But you must go back to page 7 and start again to fulfil your task.

The wizard's pet dragon has set fire to the floodgates holding back the waters of the moat. Can you see how to avoid being drowned? (See if you can grab some treasure as you float away!) But you still have to find your friends, so go back to page 7 and start again.

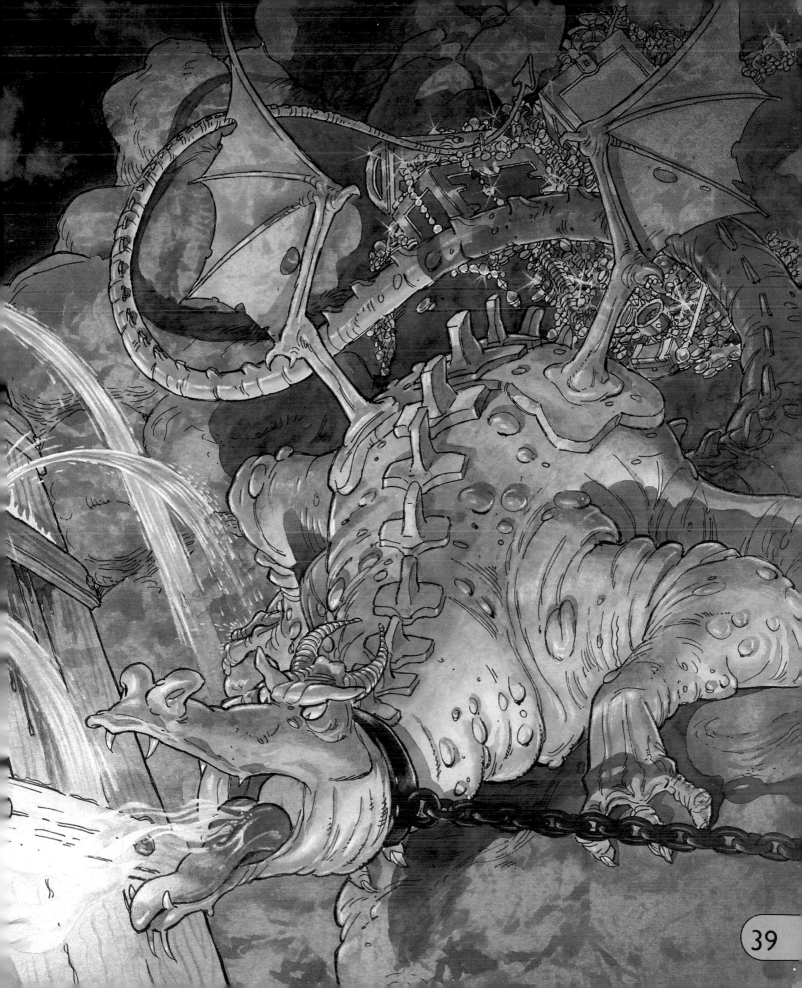

Face to face with the Slime Serpent!
Can you see how to trap it in its
watery pit for ever? But you still have
to find your friends, so go back to
page 7 and start again.

It's the wizard himself!
He's angry because Zetto
has stolen his wand. And he can't
find his pet toad. (Can you?)
While the wizard is distracted,
use the wand to magic Zetto
and yourself back to page 7
to start your quest again.

You've escaped from the castle at last! But there are wolves ahead! See which way the wind is blowing, then take the path downwind of the hungry beasts.

SAFE IN
THE VILLAGE!
YOUR TASK
IS DONE.

Answers

14
throw the grappling hook across, keeping the rope taut by tying it to one of the iron rings, and cross hand-over-hand on the rope

16
- burning fuse on cannon
- bomb in boar's mouth

- snake under dish cover
- blunderbuss in picture
- candle burning through rope will release spiked chandelier
- poison in wine bottle
- real tiger
- trap-door under chair
- dagger under table

- deadly mushrooms (fly agaric)
- deadly spider

20
an axe

24
a mallet and chisel

32
a hollow reed

34
- Zetto's medallion
- carved helmet on banister
- bat's head in arch
- pattern on beam
- shape of beam support
- battlements outside
- colour of sky
- fire in torch
- carpet on stairs

38
hop into the barrel

40
pull the chain to
dislodge the rock so
the stone slab falls
on the iron grille

44
the flag on the
castle indicates the
wind's direction